Sam's Spitfire Summer

by

Ian MacDonald

Illustrated by Charlie Clough

First Published
January 08 in Great Britain by

PUBLISHING

ISBN-10: 1-905637-43-8
ISBN-13: 978-1-905637-43-0

Educational Printing Services Limited
Albion Mill, Water Street, Great Harwood, Blackburn BB6 7QR
Telephone: (01254) 882080   Fax: (01254) 882010
E-mail: enquiries@eprint.co.uk   Website: www.eprint.co.uk

CONTENTS

Chapter 1
EVACUATION

"What's that, Grandad?"

The television was on but no one was watching. It was horse racing. The clock ticked on the mantelpiece next to the picture of Grandma Lil. Grandad had a thick book open on his lap.

"Just an album, something I used to collect when I was a boy, cigarette cards."

"I didn't know you smoked."

"I didn't. But you could get them – people left the packets lying in the road, or we swapped 'em in the playground. Got most of 'em in the war."

"Were you in the war, Grandad?"

"Well, I wasn't a soldier if that's what you mean. I was ten when the war started. I had to be evacuated, go away from home because of the bombs . . . "

Sam rubbed his hand over the train window, wiping away the mist to see out.

There were children everywhere, all wearing gas masks tied around their necks in cardboard boxes, and name labels on their collars. Some boys played chase between the rows of suitcases. Two soldiers in brown uniforms stood leaning on heavy kit bags. By Sam's window a little girl stood clutching a teddy bear.

The station guard blew his whistle. Doors banged shut as the last of the children climbed onto the train. Mums dabbed at faces with white hankies. Drifts of steam blew along the platform, hiding everything from view. And then the train began to move.

Sam pressed his face against the window. His Mum was waving, watching as the train chuff-chuffed away. Sam sat down and wiped the back of his hand across his eyes. Around him other children were laughing and chattering noisily. Didn't they

know that they were leaving their homes behind? Who knows how long they would be away!

Sam's dad had gone away too. He had run the local sweet shop. But a letter had come from the Government. And then he went away to fight the war. The Germans - it was all their fault.

"This seat free, son?"

Sam looked up. It was a soldier.

Sam nodded.

The soldier swung a large kit bag up onto the rack, and sat down facing Sam. "Busy ain't it?" he commented.

"S'pose," muttered Sam.

The soldier took out a pack of cigarettes from his pocket and opened the lid. He held them out to Sam.

"I don't . . . I'm not old enough to . . . "

"Smoke? No, they aren't ciggies. I don't smoke myself. Mug's game, I reckon." The soldier reached in with two fingers and pulled to show some cards inside. "Go on, take one."

Sam reached over and slid out one of the cards from the pack. He turned it over in his hand. On one side was some writing. On the other was a picture of a footballer in a red and white striped shirt and long white shorts.

"There you go. Stanley Matthews. The Wizard of Dribble."

Sam read the words on the back of the card and went to hand it back.

"No, keep it. I've got plenty. I collect them from me mates who smoke. All the ciggie packets have them."

Just then a group of older boys appeared from behind where the soldier was sitting. They pushed and wrestled with each other, laughing noisily as they came along the gangway. They stopped when they saw Sam.

"Here's someone all by himself," said the biggest boy.

"He's a bit posh, isn't he?" said his friend. "Look at his lovely school cap."

A third boy opened a box of matches

and took out a matchstick. He placed the head of the match on the side of the box, and flicked it with his finger. The matchstick burst into flame and flew through the air toward Sam. It landed in Sam's lap. He cried out and leapt to his feet. All the boys laughed.

"Here, cut it out." The soldier stood up. The boys looked shocked. They did not know he was there.

"I might have known!" A woman appeared, her grey hair tied tightly in a bun. "Always causing trouble. I feel sorry for those who have to look after you lot at the other end."

The boys hung their heads. The woman gave them a gentle shove in the back, and the boys moved on down the train.

"Don't worry about them," said the soldier, seeing Sam was shaken.

"It's not that," muttered Sam, "it's just I'm a bit scared of fire. I'm not very brave."

"Quite right, an' all," said the soldier. "Nasty thing fire – shouldn't be playing with matches. Nothing wrong with being scared, anyway."

"Aren't you scared, of going to fight in the war?" asked Sam.

"Me? Yeah, I'm scared alright."

"But I thought soldiers were brave."

"Well, if you do something when you're scared, I think that's brave, don't you?" said the soldier. "Now, if you haven't got any more difficult questions, I'm going to get some kip."

DID YOU KNOW?

Stanley Matthews was one of the most famous footballers of his day. He played for Stoke City, Blackpool and England in a career lasting 33 years. Playing on the right wing, and even with the heavy boots they wore then, his ball-control and speed gave him the nickname, 'The Wizard of Dribble'.

His most famous match was the cup-final of 1953. Blackpool were 3-1 down to Bolton when Stanley Matthews set off on one of his dazzling dribbles. In just half an hour Matthews had set up Stan Mortenson for an incredible hat-trick which won the game . . . and the FA Cup. The match is still called the Matthews' final to this day.

Stanley Matthews played his last game for Stoke when he was 50 years old. In 33 years of his playing career Stanley Matthews was never booked or sent off.

Facts:

Name: Stanley Matthews

Date of Birth: 1st February, 1915

Years	Clubs	Appearances	Goals
1932-47	Stoke City	259	51
1947-61	Blackpool	380	17
1961-65	Stoke City	59	3

International Career

1934-57	England	54	11

Fantastic Fact:

In the war Stanley Matthews joined the RAF, but he still found time to play football. He played as a guest for several clubs including Arsenal, Manchester United . . . and even Scotland.

Chapter 2
WELCOME TO KENT

Sam settled back in his seat and gazed out of the window.

Factories, chimneys, bridges, tunnels, stations rushed by. Now the train clattered along past rows of houses. Sam pressed his face against the glass. What were they like, the people who lived there? Were there children who did not have to go away? Were there dads too? Betty Watson's dad was a

doctor. He did not have to go to fight in
the war.

Sam turned away. Between his feet was
the brown paper bag he had been given at
the train station. He put his hand inside and
pulled out a red tin. Condensed milk. There
was a packet of biscuits, a bar of chocolate,
and some corned beef too. He put them all
back.

The train clattered on, rocking side to
side in a steady rhythm. He looked back to
the window. A woman was hanging out her
washing. She turned and waved to the train
as it sped away. Sam felt his eyelids grow
heavy.

Houses raced by and white washing
fluttered like ghosts dancing in the wind. A
footballer in a red and white striped shirt

dribbled a ball down the gangway of Sam's carriage. An enormous boy was flicking a match and the sweet shop was burning. His father's sweet shop was on fire. And he was upstairs in his bed . . . and the door was stuck . . . trying to get out . . . everywhere the smell of burning.

The train clattered over points and jolted Sam awake. He blinked and wiped a hand across his face. He was sweating. The seat opposite was empty. The soldier must have got off at an earlier station.

Sam looked down. In his hand he was still clutching the picture card. Around the edge the card was brown where the match had scorched it. Sam shivered.

He could still picture the day the sweet shop caught fire. Dad had come and they had climbed out of the window. Then Dad went back inside for Mum. He could still remember standing outside listening to the sound of the sweet jars exploding. Like bombs going off. There was nothing left afterwards. They all had to move to London. He had not been at his new school very long, not long enough to make any friends anyway. And now he was moving again. It just wasn't fair.

Sam rubbed his eyes and looked out of the window. The houses were gone.

Everywhere Sam looked there were trees, hedges and green fields. Far away, sheep were scattered like white dots on the hillside.

The train began to slow down. The other children in the carriage stood up and crowded at the window. And then the train slowed to a stop. Sam climbed on the seat and peered over the heads of two girls with pig-tails. Drifts of steam billowed by the windows making it hard to see out. Slowly the steam melted away and an empty station platform came into view.

It was nothing like the busy station he had left behind. It seemed as if they had all come to the middle of nowhere. There was not even anyone here to meet them.

"Come on everyone. Pick up your cases and get off the train, carefully now." It was the grey haired teacher Sam had seen earlier. "Not so much noise, you boys."

Children scrambled for their cases.

Sam reached up and took his down from

the luggage rack. He picked up his paper
bag from the floor. Stepping into the
gangway he was swept forward, carried along
in a tide of children. Someone turned the
handle, the door flew open and they spilled
onto the platform.

"Quiet children!" shouted a teacher.
"Line up in an orderly fashion."

The children shuffled into lines and
strained their necks to see what was going
on. Several teachers stalked up and down
making sure children behaved. And then a
woman stepped out of the crowd.

She wore a dark raincoat buckled at the
waist. On her head was a round, navy-blue
hat with a red band around the edge. In her
hand she held a clip-board. When she spoke
everyone listened, "Welcome to Kent,
children."

DID YOU KNOW?

Thousands of children were evacuated during the first week of September 1939. It was decided that children would be safer away from towns and cities when the bombing started. Every evacuee carried a gas mask and wore a name label on their coat. Here is a list of things children were told to take with them:

BOYS

2 vests
2 pairs of underpants
2 shirts
2 pairs of pyjamas
2 pairs of socks
2 pairs of boots or shoes
1 pair of wellington boots
1 coat or mackintosh
1 pair of trousers
1 pullover
6 hankies
1 toothbrush
1 face flannel
1 towel
1 comb

The list for girls was much the same except for a dress, a cardigan and a piece of underwear called a liberty bodice.

Fantastic Fact:
From September 1939 to April 1940, the expected bombing did not come. This was called the Phoney War. After months away, many homesick children returned home. Later, when the bombing really began, many children had to be evacuated for a second time.

Chapter 3
THE BILLETING OFFICER

"I am the billeting officer in charge here," said the woman. "It is my job to find you all somewhere to stay while the war is on. Now, please stay in line and follow me."

The teacher waved a hand to signal everyone to follow on. The line of children shuffled along the platform, out into a dusty lane. They walked past stone cottages with roses growing at the door; some ducks dabbled at the edge of a muddy pond; a milk cart rattled by pulled by a great white cart-horse. As the children were from the City of London, most of them had never seen a real horse.

Then, round the next corner was a white-boarded building. A sign said: Village Hall.

"Now then, make sure you're wearing your best smiles, everyone."

Sam did not know why he had to smile. Perhaps they were going to have a photograph taken.

Inside the hall were rows of wooden chairs. The lady with the blue hat spoke to one of the teachers and the children were made to sit down. Everyone began talking excitedly, wondering what would happen next.

Sam looked around at the walls of the hall. There was nothing much to see. A poster asked women to join The Land Army; a picture of the King hung on one wall; a large clock ticked slowly above the doorway.

Then the door opened and several people walked in. There was a large lady with a feather in her hat and a fur draped around her neck. She was followed close behind by a man in a grey uniform who carried a peaked cap and gloves. An older couple walked in, the man taking his hat off as he came through the door. There were three or four women on their own who all wore scarves tied over their hair. The woman in the blue hat spoke to them and they all came over to the children in turn.

First was the woman in the fur coat. Sam wondered if the man with her was her driver. He thought that she must be very rich if she could afford to buy a car, and pay someone to drive it for her.

"What about these two boys, Mrs Austin-Sykes?" said the billeting officer.

"Oh no, I don't think I could take boys. I really would not know what to do with boys," said Mrs Austin-Sykes.

"Then there's three girls here, Madam, all sisters."

The three girls smiled up at Mrs Austin Sykes, as they had been told. They wore matching coats and had their hair tied up with pink ribbon. The youngest was holding a china doll.

"Oh yes, how pretty," said Mrs Austin-

Sykes. "Emily, my housekeeper, will be able to look after them very well, I'm sure."

"Thank you, Madam."

"Well, we must do what we can for the war effort, mustn't we?"

A woman in a head-scarf chose a girl, and reluctantly agreed to take her curly-haired little brother as well. The older couple took a couple of bigger boys, saying something about work on a farm. Others arrived and did the same thing: inspecting the children, choosing who they would take.

The old clock ticked on.

And then there was no one else left.

Just Sam.

Chapter Four
PRINCESS

"I'm sorry I'm late." A tiny woman with frizzy grey hair hurried into the room.

"That's alright Mrs Hart. There's just one left."

The little, old lady seemed startled.

"Oh no, a boy! I couldn't possibly take a boy."

The billeting officer sighed and looked at her watch.

"You don't understand," the woman went on. "There's Elizabeth to think of. She's my sister's daughter up from Dover. I was hoping for a nice little girl for her to make friends with."

"Well, there's no one else, as you can see."

"I don't know what my Bert would say, if he was here."

"Your Bert would say you should do your bit for the war effort, Doris. Now come on, we haven't got all day."

The woman stood for a moment, fiddling with a wedding ring on her finger. "Oh, I suppose so. Come on then young lad. No noise, mind. I can't stand too much noise."

Sam picked up his suitcase and followed the woman out of the door.

It began to rain as they started back up the road toward the station. Two workmen at the roadside stopped to say "good morning". They were taking down road-signs. They had a cart stacked, all bearing names of places Sam had never heard of.

After a little while they turned off into a lane and came to a cottage with flowers growing in the garden.

"Hello, Aunty," said a voice.

At the gate stood a girl, about the same age as Sam. She had blonde, frizzy

hair and wore a yellow-checked dress with a white collar.

"My name's Elizabeth, what's yours?"

"Sam."

"Come on, Lillibet, let the poor boy inside. He's had a long journey."

"I thought you said your name was Elizabeth," said Sam, as he carried his suitcase inside.

"It is. Lillibet's like a nickname, like the princess, you know."

"Princess?"

"Princess Elizabeth, of course, the King's daughter," laughed the girl. "You must know that, coming from London."

"Oh, yes, of course," said Sam, turning red.

"Now, why don't you take his things

upstairs, Lillibet," said Mrs Hart. "He'll have to have the box room. I was expecting a nice little girl who could share your room, but we'll have to make do."

Sam wandered into the kitchen. A kettle was steaming on a big, black cooking range. On the table were three china cups and a plate of chocolate cake.

"Help yourself to some cake, it's homemade. I'm sure you're going to like it here," said the woman.

"Yes, I'm sure I will," said Sam, and he took a big gulp of hot tea to hide the lump in his throat. "Actually, may I . . . can you show me where the toilet is?"

"Yes, of course, dear. It's the green door, just out the back."

Sam got down from the table and went to the kitchen door. Stepping out into the back yard, he saw the brick building that was the outside toilet.

He lifted the latch and went in.

Inside, the walls were painted white. In front of him there was a dark wooden toilet seat and to the side, a small, dusty shelf. Sam sat himself down and looked up. It was just possible to see the sky through cracks in the tin roof and cobwebs hung from the walls.

As he looked around, the most enormous spider he had ever seen scuttled across the shelf. Horrified he pulled up his trousers as quickly as he could and ran back to the house.

Chapter 5
SPITFIRE

The next morning Sam was woken by a crowing noise outside his window.

He hurriedly dressed and went downstairs. Mrs Hart sat at the table holding a small, brown book.

"What's that, Aunty?" said Lillibet, washing her hands at the sink.

"My ration book . . . it came this morning."

"What's it for?"

"Well, there's not going to be so much food in the shops, it seems. It says how much you can have each week, see?" She pointed to a page which was printed with squares and numbers. "Still, at least there's fresh eggs this morning."

After a tasty breakfast of bacon, eggs, toast and homemade jam, Sam followed Lillibet outside into a long, narrow garden. A little path wound its way down through a tumble of flowers. Then, beyond a hedge, several kinds of green plants poked out of the ground in neat rows.

"That's Aunty's vegetable patch," said

Lillibet. "There's carrots, cabbage, and Aunty's prize onions."

And then, beyond another hedge, a surprise – several chickens inside a wire fence.

Lillibet handed Sam a small bucket of seed which they both sprinkled on the ground. Sam crouched down. He watched as the chickens rushed about, scratching at the ground for the seed.

"What are they for?" he asked.

"What do you think, stupid? They lay eggs – that's what we had for breakfast, remember? And we have chicken for dinner, sometimes."

Sam made a face.

"Well, where do you think your Sunday lunch comes from?" laughed Lillibet. And she stood up and ran towards a tiny gate at the bottom of the garden. Sam followed, and in a moment they were out into fields and woods and trees.

"Come on, I'll race you," shouted Lillibet.

Sam ran as hard as he could, but Lillibet was a fast runner. She was soon across an open field and into the wood, skipping in and out of trees and jumping fallen logs like an athlete.

Then, just as quickly, they were out of the woods and running up a hill. Lillibet hardly seemed to slow at all. In minutes she was at the top. Sam stopped half-way up, panting. Lillibet picked up a stick and waved it madly, like someone waving a flag on a castle.

'I can't be beaten by a girl,' thought Sam, and he started to run again, pumping his arms hard to help him climb.

At the top he fell and lay on his back

looking up at the sky. Lillibet flopped down beside him. They lay there just watching the white clouds drifting over the downs. And then there was the sound of an engine overhead and an aeroplane swooped across the sky.

It was painted in green and brown patches with red and blue circles on the end of its wings.

"A Spitfire!" shouted Sam, jumping to his feet.

"How do you know?" said Lillibet, shielding her eyes against the sun.

"The round wings, look."

They both watched as the plane climbed high into the clouds. And then it turned and began to spin, faster and faster, speeding toward the ground.

"It's going to crash," gasped Lillibet.

"No it isn't," said Sam. "Watch!"

Then, just when it seemed as if it was going

to hit the ground, the Spitfire straightened up, climbing again in a great loop, back into the clouds.

"He's putting on a show, just for us," said Lillibet, and she waved wildly.

Sam laughed.

"Race you back," he shouted, and set off before Lillibet was ready.

DID YOU KNOW?

When war started in September 1939 food was in short supply. Food had to be rationed, which meant that people could only buy a set amount each week.

Everyone was given a ration book which allowed you to buy your weekly amount.

Here is one week's ration for one adult:

100g of bacon and ham
50g butter
50g cheese
100g margarine
100g cooking fat
3 pints milk
50g tea
225g sugar
1 egg

Fantastic Fact:
Even the royal family had their own ration book.

Chapter 6
COWS

"Neeaaoow!"

Sam put both arms out and charged down the hill.

"Spitfire's scrambled . . . bandits at 9-o-clock. Neeaaoow! Prepare to fire . . . ack-ack-ack."

Sam dipped his arms as he swooped around and disappeared under the trees.

He skipped over branches and ran in and out of the trees. He could hear the sound of footsteps behind him. Lillibet must be catching up.

Then, something hard thudded into his back, and he fell forward. Sam felt several hands grab his jumper, and he was rolled over onto his back. Before he could get a glimpse of his attackers, wet leaves were thrust into his face. More hands pulled at his jumper and more leaves were pushed inside.

"Yah, Townie! Here's a bit of the countryside for you."

And just as quickly, they ran off and disappeared into the trees.

"Are you O.K.?" asked Lillibet, running to where Sam lay.

"Yes, I think so."

Sam stood up and shook the leaves out of his jumper. Lillibet picked some bits of twig from his hair.

"Who were they?"

"I don't know. It was all too quick. Anyway, shouldn't we be getting back?"

"Yes, come on. Aunty will be making tea soon."

Sam and Lillibet walked on through the woods.

When they came to the fields again it was full of cows munching on grass. Lillibet kept on walking but Sam stopped still. He had only ever seen cows in books. These animals looked like monsters. Some of them even had horns. Lillibet was already half way across the field.

"Come on, Sam, we'll be late for tea."

Sam looked at Lillibet, and then at the cows. One of the cows decided to move forward onto the path. It looked across at Sam, grass and spittle dribbling from its mouth. Just then, a baby calf nearby made a bleating sound, and the cow on the path mooed loudly.

Sam stepped back.

"Come on, Sam. They won't hurt you."

Sam stepped forward slowly, and took a few paces towards the great animal. It looked up at him. Sam stepped nearer, and the animal lumbered off the path. Sam hurried on and joined Lillibet.

When they got to Mrs Hart's back gate there were three boys standing there.

"Hello, Townie. Had a nice walk, have you?"

The biggest boy had a grass stalk sticking from his mouth like a cigarette.

"Hope the nasty cows haven't scared you!"

The other boys laughed. The laughter sounded familiar.

"Had fun playing in the leaves, then?"

"Very funny," said Lillibet, "come on, Sam." And she walked forward, brushing past the largest of the boys as she stepped through the gate. Sam followed.

"See you at school, Townie. We'll be waiting for you."

Chapter 7
SCHOOL

The playground was noisy. Three boys were playing "tag". Others stood in groups sharing stories about the places they were billeted.

Sam stood at the edge looking on. He hardly knew anyone. And, for some reason, Elizabeth had been put down to go in the afternoon, with the children from the village.

A bell rang and everyone lined up. Several teachers appeared.

"Line up here, quietly now. Little ones here, juniors in this line."

The children lined up and filed into the building. They went straight into a small hall and Mr Peters, who Sam recognised from London, stood up on a stage and spoke.

"Good morning children. We are very grateful to the headmaster for making us all welcome." He paused to look at a man in a grey suit who was sitting behind.

The man nodded.

"We are to be allowed to use the school building in the mornings, while the village children will come in the afternoons. I'm sure that you will be able to find things to amuse you after lunch (he paused and one or two children laughed, politely). But, please remember that we are guests here, so don't go making a nuisance of yourselves out of school."

Then Mr Peters read out the names of the classes and their teachers. Sam was in Mr Peters' class with the older children. The younger juniors were being looked after by Miss Nunn, with the infants all together with Mrs Page.

The day began with prayers, some reading and chanting the times tables. Then everyone had to write about their journey to Kent.

At lunchtime the children spilled out into the sunshine, excited at the thought of the whole afternoon to themselves. Some of the children from the village were beginning to arrive for afternoon school.

"Why don't we go and see the animals?" said one of the boys who was billeted at Scott's farm. Sam had nothing else to do, so he followed on a little way behind the group. The walk took them down a lane, past the big house where the Jenkins girls were staying, and along by a stream that trickled by a row of thatched cottages.

Further on, Sam stopped to watch some women loading hay onto carts. Soon, the rest of the group were quite a way in front of him.

"Hello, Townie. You're going the wrong way."

Three boys blocked the path.

"I'm just going to the farm to see the horses," said Sam.

"Is that right, Townie? Well, I meant you're going the wrong way, 'cos London's back there. That's where you belong, isn't it?"

The biggest boy with the freckles and red braces took Sam's cap off and tossed it over the nearest fence. Sam watched it go. On the other side of the fence was a cow.

"Go on then, Townie. You're not scared of the moo-cow, are you?"

"Steady on, Bob. That's going a bit far isn't it?" said one of the others.

"No, let's see what the townie's made of. Go on. See if you can get it back."

Sam looked at the boys, and then into the field. The big cow was standing some way from his cap.

What would Lillibet think if I tell her I was scared of a cow again, thought Sam? He looked back at the boys who were watching to see what he would do. He made up his mind.

He climbed up so that he was sitting on top of the fence. Then he lowered himself slowly to the ground. The animal turned its head. It was black, and had large curved horns and a ring through its nose. It was enormous.

Sam took three steps forward. The great beast turned and faced Sam. It lowered its head. With its front hoof it pawed the ground.

"SAM! NO! IT'S A BULL!"

It was Elizabeth's voice.

Sam turned.

When he looked again the huge
creature was charging towards him. Sam
forgot about his cap and began to run. He
took a flying leap and grabbed at the top of
the fence. Swinging his legs over, he fell in a
heap on the grass.

The fence shuddered as the bull
clattered into it.

DID YOU KNOW?

Women had a very important part to play in World War Two Britain. Up until then it had been thought that it was a man's job to go to work, and that women should stay at home to look after the children and do the housework. The war changed all that. When the war began men went away to fight and women now had to do all jobs the men left behind.

Here are just some of the jobs they had to do:

Factory Worker -
Many women went to work in factories making weapons, parachutes or machinery needed for the troops overseas. To keep everyone happy the factories often played music and the workers sang along.

'Land Girl' -
The Women's Land Army sent women out to work on the farms. They carried out heavy work such as ploughing, turning hay and

looking after the animals. They soon became known as the 'Land Girls'.

Nurse -
Women were needed to work abroad and at home caring for the injured. This might be a soldier returning from the war, or someone who had been trapped under the rubble of a bombed house.

Wren -
Thousands of women did join the armed forces, though not always to fight. They could do office work, drive army trucks or be a motorbike messenger. Women who joined the navy were called WRENS after the Women's Royal Naval Service (WRNS).

Spy -
Some women went abroad to act as spies,
often working in secret behind enemy lines.
Other women were put to work decoding
secret spy messages picked up on the radio.

WVS -
A different king of organisation that women
could join was called the Women's Voluntary
Service. They did unpaid work looking after
evacuees, helping those who had been bombed
out of their homes or just making cups of tea
to cheer people up.

Fantastic Fact:
In 1942 Princess Elizabeth signed up to do
her war service at the age of sixteen.

Chapter 8
BOMB SHELTER

Sam's first week seemed to last forever.

The second week seemed to pass more quickly. Sam tried to keep out of the way of Bob Trotter and his gang.

One day, returning from morning school, Sam came home to find a lorry outside the cottage. Two men were unloading sheets of metal.

"What's going on, Aunty?"

"It's an Anderson Shelter, Sam." She handed him a leaflet from the table. Inside were some diagrams and instructions. "Not that the Germans are going to drop bombs here. Don't worry, they'll bomb London before us." Mrs Hart bit her lip. It was a stupid thing to say. "Now, why don't you go out and give Mr Chambers a hand?"

Sam went out into the garden and there was Mr Chambers from next door. He was leaning on a shovel, a cup of tea in his hand. He stood in his vest, braces hanging loosely at his side. He was not a young man, but he had worked on the farms all his life and still looked strong. Already Mr Chambers had cut away a large rectangle of grass from the lawn.

"Come to give me a hand, Sam? There's a spade there."

Mr Chambers showed Sam how to put a foot on the spade to dig into the soil, and then how to throw it onto a pile. "Throw it far enough away. We don't want it falling back into the hole."

Sam started digging, but after half-an-hour sweat was pouring down his back.

"You've got too much on, lad," laughed Mr Chambers.

Sam looked back at the house. Lillibet would be home from school soon. He did not want to be seen in his vest, but there was nothing else for it. He took off his jumper and unbuttoned his shirt.

They carried on for a while, not wasting energy talking. Sam lost track of time but, when Elizabeth came home, he knew it must be just after 4 o'clock.

"What's going on?" said Lillibet, shocked. "Why are you digging up Aunty's lawn?"

"It's an air-raid shelter," said Sam.

"It's got to go here," said Mr Chambers. "You've got to be able to get to it quickly when the siren goes."

"Time for a break, everyone," said Mrs Hart, appearing with a jug and glasses. "Homemade lemonade!"

When the hole was deep enough, Mr Chambers went home for his tea and promised to come back to put the shelter together.

Later that evening Sam held each section in place while Mr Chambers bolted the whole thing together.

Soon there was a metal tunnel standing in the hole. More panels were fixed to the ends and a doorway was added facing the house.

Then, using the earth from the hole, they covered the shelter with more than a foot of soil.

In the next couple of days Mr Chambers returned and built bunk beds down each side. Lillibet and Sam enjoyed fitting the shelter out with blankets, a little card table from indoors and a gas lamp.

"That looks just fine," said Mrs Hart. "Let's just hope we never have to use it!"

DID YOU KNOW?

During the war people needed to be protected from the threat of bombs. Special shelters were supplied to every house. These were made up of several sheets of corrugated (wavy) metal which had to be bolted together. They were called **Anderson Shelters** after Sir John Anderson, the minister in charge. When the air-raid sounded everyone had to climb out of their warm beds and rush to the shelter.

Here is how to put together your Anderson Shelter:

Measurements:

Height	6foot	(1.8m)
Width	$4^1/_2$foot	(1.4m)
Length	$6^1/_2$foot	(2m)

1.   Begin by digging a rectangular hole 3 feet deep (about a metre). Make it long and wide enough to fit your shelter.
2.   Next, stand the metal pieces in the hole and bolt them together to form a kind of tunnel.

3. Fix on the ends. Make sure the door is nearest the house!
4. Cover the whole thing with at least 15 inches of earth (using the earth from the hole that you dug to begin with).
5. Kit your shelter out by building bunk beds for all the family. You may need a bucket in the corner for . . . guess what?
6. Grow vegetables on top of your shelter to help with those nasty food rations.

Fantastic Fact:
Many people in London used the underground train stations to shelter from the bombs instead. People slept anywhere they could, on platforms, on the stairs and escalators, or even on hammocks hung from the walls.

Chapter 9
MR POTTS

"Open your exercise books everyone."
Mr Peters wrote the date on the board.
Tuesday 23rd July 1940.
"Now turn to page 14 in your history book.
Today we are going to learn about Julius
Caesar. You can begin by copying the passage
at the top of the page."

Nibs clinked in ink wells. Children began
to write. Sam looked around the classroom.

He could hardly believe that he had been here a whole school year. Over the months some of the homesick evacuees had gone home. The bombing had not been as bad as everyone expected. But Sam's mum would not let him go back. They had not been given Anderson Shelters for nothing.

Now, with fewer children in the village, the older ones could be taught in one class. Thirty two children packed into rows was a bit of a squeeze, but at least they could now stay the whole day. This pleased the grown-ups who were fed-up with the Londoners getting up to mischief in the afternoons.

"Bother!" Sam looked down at his book. There was a large blob of ink in the middle of his page.

"Sam, why are you out of your seat?"

"I'm just getting some blotting paper, Sir," said Sam.

Mr Peters tutted and returned to the pile of arithmetic books on the tall desk.

Sam picked up a sheet of pink paper and looked out of the window. Above the downs, was a single aeroplane. Sam stood watching for a moment as it climbed into a clear blue sky.

A Spitfire.

Just then the door opened, and Sam went back to his seat.

"Good Morning, Mr Potts," said Mr Peters, getting up to shake hands.

"Good Morning, Mr Peters," said Mr

Potts, taking off a helmet with A.R.P. in white letters on the front. "May I have a word with the children?"

"Yes, of course," said Mr Peters. "Put down your pens children and pay attention."

The uniformed man strode to the front of the classroom.

"You all know who I am, the Air Raid Patrol Warden. I check your blackouts and sound the air raid, and the like."

Some of the children nodded. The warden had been to their houses to check they had no lights showing at night. If you had, there was a heavy fine to pay. No one liked Mr Potts very much.

"This morning I've come to talk to you about a very serious matter. As you know, there's been dog-fights over the village during the last couple of weeks . . . "

"That means aeroplanes," added Mr Peters.

"That's correct, and sometimes there are bits off aeroplanes that drop out of the sky. Shrapnel is what it's called. Anyway, there's been reports of children picking up shrapnel, and taking it home." He paused. "Now, that's dangerous for a start. Shrapnel can still be hot and you can get a nasty burn. Besides, it's against the law, and you can get yourself in serious trouble."

"If you find anything," added Mr Peters, "you should report it to Mr Potts right away."

"Please, Sir."

"What is it, Bob?" said Mr Peters.

"I know where there is some."

"What are you talking about, lad?" said Mr Potts.

"Some shrapnel. I know where there is some."

Bob Trotter got out of his seat and went and stood beside Sam's desk.

He reached forward and lifted the wooden lid.

Sam gasped.

DID YOU KNOW?

To make it difficult for enemy bombers to spot the towns below, everyone had to make sure there was no light showing from their houses. This was called the blackout. People used curtains, sheets or paper to cover every window in the house.

❑ The blackout began on the 1st September, 1939.

❑ Air Raid Patrol wardens checked up on houses and factories to make sure they had no lights showing. If any light could be seen from outside you could face a heavy fine.

❑ Street lamps were turned off and car headlights had to be covered. About 4000 people died as a result of traffic accidents during the blackout.

❑ A government leaflet advised men to hang their white shirt-tails out over their trousers so that drivers would spot them on the dark roads.

❑ Many drowned during the blackout as people fell off bridges, blundered into ponds or tumbled into rivers.

❑ In Denham, Buckinghamshire, one man was badly injured when he stepped from a train. He thought the train had stopped at the station . . . but it was only waiting for the signal to change. He fell 80 feet over the edge of a high bridge.

Fantastic Fact:
Farmers were afraid their cows might be hit by cars in the blackout . . . so they painted them with bright, white stripes!

"I say, old chap, are those cows or zebras on the road ahead!?"

Chapter 10
SHRAPNEL

There, inside his desk, was a jumble of nuts and bolts and bits of metal.

Mr Peters got down from his desk and walked over, followed by the A.R.P. warden.

"Sam?" said Mr Peters, a puzzled look on his face.

Sam looked up. Bob Trotter was

standing behind the large figure of Mr Potts. He was grinning all over his face. Silently, he mouthed one word back at Sam, 'Townie'.

"I know about you London lot," said the A.R.P. Warden. "A right bunch of thieving rascals, I've heard."

Sam blinked back the tears. It was no use trying to explain. They would not believe a word. He was a Londoner. He did not belong here.

"I think you better come with me, young fellah."

Suddenly, Sam felt the anger well up inside like a hot ball of fire. He stood up, knocking over his chair. Bursting forward, he pushed between the two men and made a dive for Bob Trotter. The large boy gave a yelp as a fist caught him on the ear. Sam bolted for the door.

"Just leave me alone," he yelled back. "I didn't ask to come here, anyway."

He slammed the door hard just as the A.R.P. warden rushed forward to make a grab for him.

Sam burst out into the playground. He pushed open the school gate and began to run. He had no idea where he was going. He just ran.

Turning a corner, he bumped into a milkman carrying a crate. Bottles clattered to the ground, broken glass rolled across the road, white milk spilled into the gutter. Sam rolled over, bits of glass sticking to his shorts.

He picked himself up and hurried on.
Soon the houses were left behind and Sam
stumbled into the coolness of the wood.

Out of the sun he was blinded for a
moment, and he blundered into a tree,
banging his shoulder. But still he ran, and

out into the hot sun again, now climbing, climbing until he fell on his back at last, panting in the long grass. Sam lay still watching the white clouds drift by.

And there, above his head was his Spitfire.

He stood, to get a better look. It swooped low over his head. Sam saw the familiar green and brown splodges on the tail, and the red and blue circles on the wings.

Sam waved.

The plane dipped its wing, almost as if in salute. Sam watched as the plane arched upwards, disappearing into the white clouds above. Then it appeared again, diving towards him with a deafening roar.

But something was different. The plane was a different colour. Grey. And at the end of each wing was a black cross.

A German fighter plane!

A Messerschmitt.

DID YOU KNOW?

The Spitfire was one of the most successful fighter planes of World War Two. It was used in the Battle of Britain from 10th July to 31st October, 1939. The British RAF fought against the German air-force, the Luftwaffe, over the South Coast. The RAF had to defeat the Luftwaffe to stop Hitler from carrying out his plan to invade Britain.

Here are some facts about the amazing Spitfire:

Type	Fighter
Designer	R. J. Mitchell
Crew	1
Top Speed	408mph (656Km/h)
Fire Power	8 machine guns
Number made	20,351
Used by	RAF (Royal Air Force)
Main opponent	Messerschmitt BF 109

Fantastic Fact:
The new Spitfire planes had a new invention - wheels that slid back inside the plane after take-off. There were sometimes accidents because the first test pilots kept forgetting to put their wheels back out again to land!

Chapter 11
GREY ANGEL

Just as quickly the Spitfire came into view again, looping down into the path of the oncoming German. Sam watched, unable to move, as the two planes flew head on. There was a crackle of noise and trails of bright fire shot from both planes. Sam knew he was watching a deadly battle.

Then, when it seemed that the two planes would crash, the Spitfire dipped one wing and wheeled away to the left. Now the German arched his plane upwards, climbing into the cover of the cloud. The Spitfire made a steep turn, and headed back.

Now the green and brown of the British plane headed up into the clouds. For a moment, neither plane could be seen. There was another burst of gunfire and the Spitfire appeared, the German fighter closely on its tail.

Sam gasped.

A thin wisp of black smoke showed on the Spitfire. The plane, its trail of dark smoke behind it, headed downward. The Messerschmitt closed in, guns firing. At the last moment, the Spitfire pulled out of its dive and climbed again into the cloud. The German followed. Sam knew that the

Spitfire was in trouble. The Messerschmitt was close on its tail and the Spitfire had already taken a hit.

Sam watched and waited.

Suddenly, an enormous shape filled the sky above him.

Sam fell backwards as the great underbelly of the plane thundered over his head. The air around him became suddenly hot. Smoke filled his eyes and nostrils and the sound of the engine threatened to deafen him.

Sam looked down the hill as the fighter plane disappeared into the trees below. And then there was the sound of an explosion and crashing and tearing . . . and then it was quiet.

There were two wisps of grey smoke where the plane had come down. Where there was smoke there was fire. Sam wanted to turn and run away, but he knew that there could be a Spitfire pilot who might be badly injured and needed his help. There was no one else.

Half falling, half running, Sam headed down the hill and into the woods. The smell of burning was everywhere. He ran in and out of the trees heading towards the smoke.

And then he saw it.

A dark grey shape hanging, nose down in a tree.

The Messerschmitt!

Sam stopped dead.

There, caught in a tree next to the broken plane, was a German airman. A white parachute was spread out behind him. He looked like a grey angel.

The trapped pilot was only yards away. Sam could reach him in seconds. There was the sound of a small explosion and the Messerschmitt slipped further down the tree. Fuel was seeping from the engine. Flames began to lick their way across the ground towards the trailing strings of the parachute. The plane gave another loud crack and part of the propeller fell away. It was like a sound Sam had heard before. The sound of sweet jars exploding.

Sam hesitated, too scared to move.

Chapter 12
"HELP ME"

A voice spoke.

"Helfen sie mir, bitte." *Help me, please.*

But in his head Sam could hear other voices.

He could hear his mother screaming his name as the sweet jars exploded. The voices of the children on the playground.

The soldier on the train.

Sam!

Townie! Townie! You don't belong here.

Fire!

I didn't ask to come here, anyway!

Help!

If you do something when you're scared, I think that's brave, don't you?

Help me, please!

And then there was another voice at his shoulder.

"Help, Sam, help him! Do something!"
It was Lillibet.

"Why should I?" Sam felt the tears hot in his eyes. "Why should I help him? He's a German. He's the reason my dad's gone away . . . why I've had to leave my home!"

"Sam," shouted Lillibet, "he didn't ask to come here, either."

Sam looked up at the trapped airman. 'He is hardly more than a boy. He didn't ask to be here either. He's no different to me', Sam thought.

Like waking from a dream, he started into action. He raced across the ground and hurled himself against the tree trunk. The bark was slippery, but he clung on. Reaching up, he grabbed the first branch and began to climb. His arms ached as he pulled himself closer to the trapped airman.

When he reached the place where the German hung, he jammed one foot into a V in the branches and leaned across. He had seen pictures of parachutes in books and knew that the release buckle was somewhere in front. He found it and banged hard.

Nothing happened. He banged again. Still nothing.

Sam looked down. There were flames now at the foot of the tree. If he stayed any longer he might be burned alive. Then he remembered the broken glass. He put a hand in his pocket. His fingers found something sharp. He tugged. The glass was stuck firm. A trickle of blood oozed down his fingers. He tried again. This time it came free.

Sam reached up and sawed the cords of the parachute. It seemed to take forever, but one by one they cut through. Then, with a cry of pain, the German fell forward, and crashed on to the ground below.

Sam scrambled down and, with Lillibet's help, they dragged the man away from the burning tree.

The airman looked at Sam and smiled.

"Danke. Danke, meine Freund," he breathed.

"Danke? Does that mean thank you in German?"

"That's right. Thank you, my friend," said Grandad.

Grandad put the picture of Stanley Matthews back in the album and closed the book.

"And what happened to the other man, the Spitfire pilot?"

"I don't know. I think he must have limped back to base. There were several airfields nearby. Least, I hope that's what happened."

"And, after the war, did you ever see Lillibet again?"

"See her?" Grandad laughed. He lifted the photo from the mantelpiece and gave it a polish with his sleeve. "I thought you'd worked it out," he smiled, blinking at misty eyes. "Lillibet, that's your Grandma. Grandma Lil."

"But I always thought Lil was short for Lily."

"No, lad. Lillibet. Elizabeth, like the Queen."

DID YOU KNOW?

Princess Elizabeth was 13 years old when war broke out in 1939. Her family played an important part in leading their country through difficult times. She was known as Lillibet by her family and the British people too. Princess Elizabeth later became Queen Elizabeth II.

❏ Elizabeth's father was King George VI and the Queen was also called Elizabeth. George VI had been King for three years when war broke out. Princess Elizabeth had a younger sister called Margaret.

❏ When the war began the Royal Family continued to live at Buckingham Palace, facing the threat of German bombs. In 1940, the princesses were moved to Windsor Castle, not far away, where their parents came to stay with them at week-ends.

❑ Princess Elizabeth, aged 14, made her first radio broadcast on 13th October 1940. She spoke to children across the country on BBC's *Children's Hour* telling them that, "in the end . . . all will be well."

❑ At 16 years of age Princess Elizabeth turned up to register for War Service in her Girl Guide uniform. She was told that she was too young to "join-up".

❑ Later, aged 18, Princess Elizabeth joined the ATS where she learned to drive and look after car engines. By this time the fighting was nearly over and she did not have to play an active part in the war.

Fantastic Fact:
Buckingham Palace suffered nine direct hits from German bombs during the war. But still the Royal Family did not budge!

Also available in the Reluctant Reader Series from:

PUBLISHING

The Curse of the Full Moon *(Mystery)*
Stephanie Baudet   ISBN 978 1 904904 11 3

A Marrow Escape *(Adventure)*
Stephanie Baudet   ISBN 1 900818 82 5

The One That Got Away *(Humorous)*
Stephanie Baudet   ISBN 1 900818 87 6

The Haunted Windmill *(Mystery)*
Margaret Nash   ISBN 978 1 904904 22 9

Friday the Thirteenth *(Humorous)*
David Webb   ISBN 978 1 905637 37 9

Trevor's Trousers *(Humorous)*
David Webb   ISBN 978 1 904904 19

The Library Ghost *(Mystery)*
David Webb   ISBN 978 1 904374 66

Dinosaur Day *(Adventure)*
David Webb   ISBN 978 1 904374 67 1

Laura's Game *(Football)*
David Webb   ISBN 1 900818 61 2

Grandma's Teeth *(Humorous)*
David Webb   ISBN 978 1 905637 20 1

The Curse of the Pharaoh's Tomb
                          (Egyptian Adventure)
David Webb   ISBN 978 1 905637 42 3

The Bears Bite Back *(Humorous)*
Derek Keilty   ISBN 978 1 905637 36 2

Order online @ **www.eprint.co.uk**